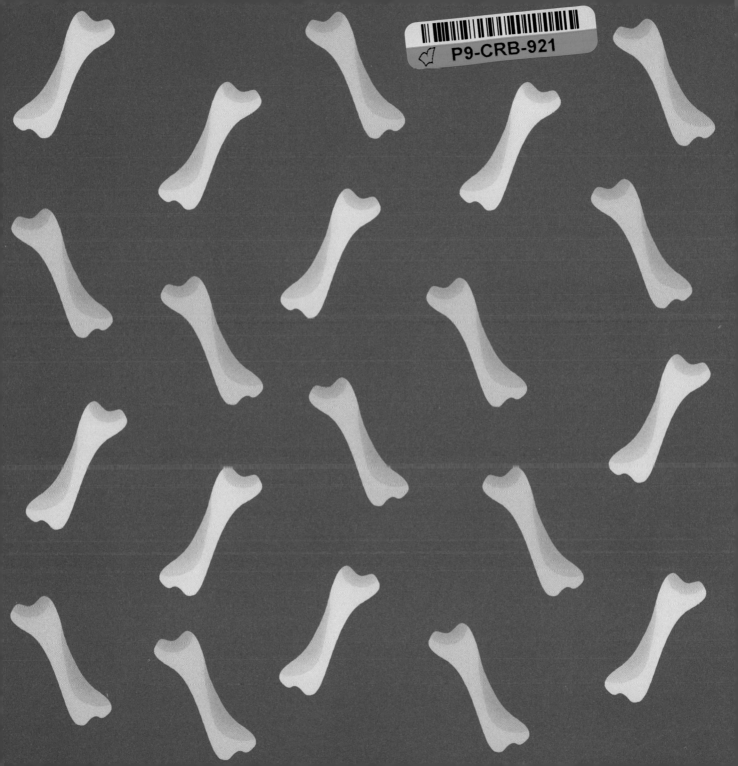

P9-CRB-921

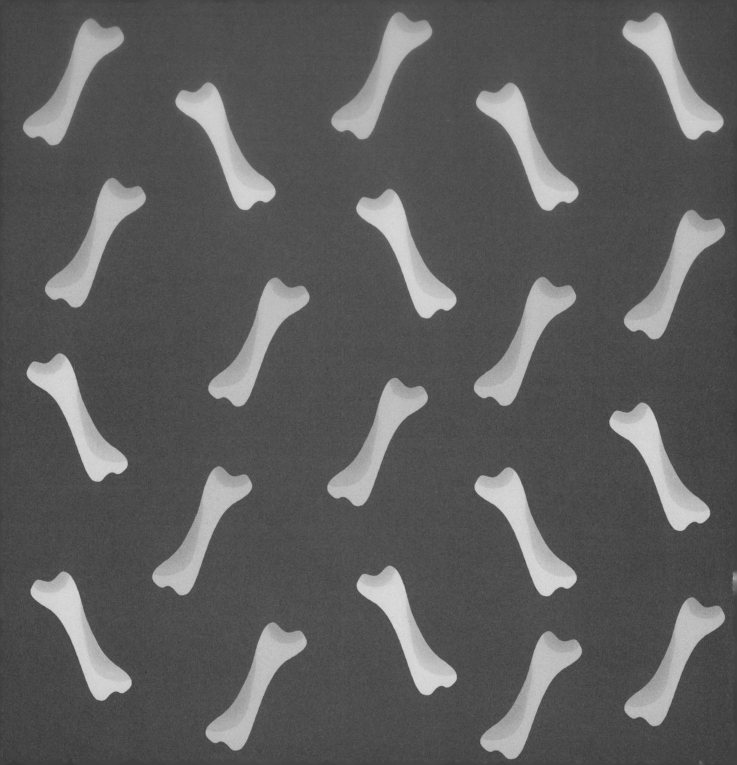

Curious George®

Museum Mystery

Adaptation by Anna Meier
Based on the TV series teleplay written by Joe Fallon

Houghton Mifflin Harcourt
Boston   New York

Curious George television series merchandise © 2017 Universal Studios. Curious George and related characters, created by Margret and H. A. Rey, are copyrighted and registered by Houghton Mifflin Harcourt Publishing Company and used under license. Licensed by Universal Studios Licensing LLC. All rights reserved. The PBS KIDS logo is a registered trademark of PBS and is used with permission.

For information about permission to reproduce selections from this book, write to Permissions, Houghton Mifflin Harcourt Publishing Company, 3 Park Avenue, 19th Floor, New York, New York, 10016.

ISBN: 978-0-544-85992-0 paper over board
ISBN: 978-0-544-86707-9 paperback
Design by Lauren Pettapiece
Cover art adaptation by Artful Doodlers Ltd.
www.hmhco.com
Printed in China
SCP 10 9 8 7 6 5 4 3 2 1
4500638661

It was a big day at the museum. A new dinosaur skeleton was going to be displayed. George was always a curious little monkey, and he was especially curious about dinosaurs.

"At five o'clock, the museum will be filled with dinosaur experts waiting to see the new skeleton on stage," Professor Wiseman told George and the man with the yellow hat, "but I'm one bone short!"

"Isn't that one of the bones we brought to you last week?" the man asked.
"It should have been," the professor said, "but there were only three bones
in this box. There were supposed to be four. Are you sure you put all the
bones in that box?"

George remembered that their friend Mr. Quint had been visiting and taking pictures. They could look at those photos to solve the mystery of the missing bone. He and his friend went home to look for the pictures.

George found Mr. Quint's photos of his visit to the city. There were two pictures of the man with the box.

"Look, George. The box was too full to close at home. But it was closed tightly when we reached the museum," the man said. "That means there was less inside when we dropped it off. We must have lost the bone somewhere along the way."

"To find it, we should retrace our steps," the man told George. But George couldn't remember their exact path to the museum.

Luckily, they had more pictures! George put them in a photo holder.
"If we put the pictures in order, we can retrace our path and find that
bone!" the man exclaimed.

George thought the first place they'd gone was Chef Pisghetti's restaurant for soup. They went to Pisghetti's and showed him the picture Mr. Quint had taken.

Looking at the photo closely, Pisghetti noticed a clue. "There's the box, right next to your bag from the market!" George hadn't noticed the bag.

"The market bag means we must have gone to the market before we came here," the man said. He changed the order of the photos in George's holder so the picture from the market came before the picture from Pisghetti's. They set off to check the market for clues.

"Remember, we almost lost all the bones here when you tripped," the man reminded George. But George, being a quick little monkey, had caught all four of them in the box.

"Still four bones," the man with the yellow hat said.

Now he and George looked closely at the other pictures. The man noticed that George had a noodle on his cheek in the next picture at the lake. "George, this means we had soup before we went to the park!" he said.

They thought they remembered their path now. They left home, went to the market, then went to Pisghetti's for soup, stopped at the park, and then delivered the box to the museum.

The box was still bulging in the picture from the park, so the lost bone had to be somewhere between the park and the museum. The pictures had to be in the right order, didn't they? But George noticed something else. George's friend had fallen into the lake at the park, but his clothes were dry in the picture at the museum. "That's right!" his friend exclaimed. "We went home again for dry clothes." The lobby wasn't just the first step on their path—it was also the next-to-last step.

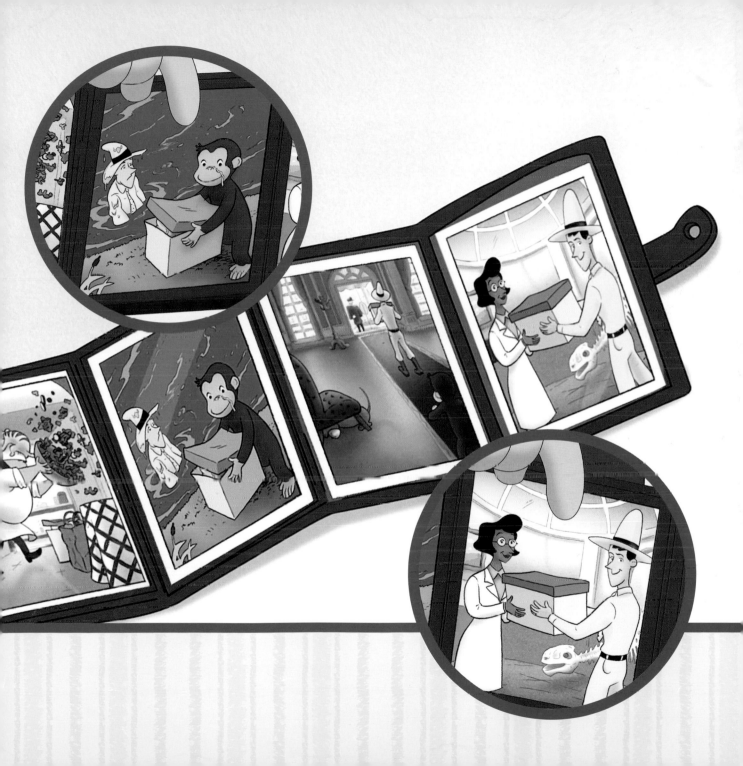

They hurried back home to ask the doorman if he remembered anything about that day. "Sure, I remember! You left the box in the lobby while you changed. Then your friend took this picture as you left in the dry clothes," he told them.

George noticed something else in the picture. What was that white blur under the chair with the doorman's dog? George went to find Hundley. When he found Hundly he also found . . . the bone!

They had the missing bone, but it was almost five o'clock! George and his friend ran back to the museum and put the bone in its place just in time. "Let's go!" the man whispered.

But his pants were caught in the Ankylosaurus's mouth!

The curtains opened, and the audience got an even bigger surprise than they expected! George had solved the mystery and saved Dr. Wiseman's big reveal at the museum! Plus, now he had a new photo to add to his collection.

Retrace your steps!

George's friend Mr. Quint took pictures of everything they did on the day of his visit. You can retrace your own steps too. All you'll need are some pictures of yourself at different points throughout the day.

Have a parent or friend take pictures of you doing different activities on a single day or ask for paper and crayons and draw your own pictures of your activities.

The next day, scramble up these pictures and use the clues you see in each one to put them in the correct order! When you're finished you can put these pictures in an existing journal or scrapbook, or use them to start a new one!

Which comes first?

George's friends helped him find clues in each of Mr. Quint's pictures. These clues helped George and the man with the yellow hat figure out what happened first, next, and last throughout their day.

Looking at the pictures below of George planting a seed, can you put them in the correct order?

A   ## B   ## C   ## D

Answer key: C, D, A, B